Dragons HATE To Be Discreet

Alfred A. Knopf  New York

Dragons HATE To Be Discreet

A Story by
WINIFRED ROSEN

Pictures by
EDWARD KOREN

For the Garbers
who have been through it all
and survived

THIS IS A BORZOI BOOK PUBLISHED BY ALFRED A. KNOPF, INC.

Text Copyright © 1978 by Winifred Rosen. Illustrations Copyright © 1978 by Edward Koren. All rights reserved
under International and Pan-American Copyright Conventions. Published in the United States by Alfred A. Knopf,
Inc., New York, and simultaneously in Canada by Random House of Canada Limited, Toronto. Distributed by
Random House, Inc., New York. Manufactured in the United States of America. 10 9 8 7 6 5 4 3 2 1
(CIP data located on last page)

Inside this book is a dragon.
But don't worry. She won't bite unless I tell her to.
And I promise I won't tell her to bite you.

Only just please remember to stand back when she breathes her fire. Except when she's breathing fire, she isn't even too dangerous.

You probably want to know how I got her, but if I told you the truth you wouldn't believe it. Because the truth is, I didn't get her. The truth is, she got me.

Anyhow, now we've got each other.

Most of the time my dragon is invisible to most people. Oh, it's not that she's some kind of fake, made-up or *pretend* dragon, it's just that my dragon can make herself into any shape you can think of and stay that way for as long as you like.

Even my mother sometimes forgets she's around.
But she always is—wound around some piece of the furniture—appearing to be part of the décor.

Waiting . . .

If you want to know what she's waiting for, I'll tell you. She's waiting for the Right Moment to come along. Whenever the Right Moment comes along, she becomes the True Dragon that she really is.

It is disturbing to most people (especially my mother) when a True Dragon explodes into life, breathing fire. But that's what happens.

Here's how.

We're having breakfast, say, and I'm annoyed because we've run out of the only cereal I happen to feel like eating.

My father's annoyed because he's reading the morning paper. The paper always annoys him, which must be the reason he reads it.

My mother's annoyed because nobody's helping her with anything and the cat's clawed a run in her stocking. She says several of those words you're not ever supposed to say, especially in front of children, and glares at the cat.

I giggle.

"Some joke!" my mother cries.

I say, "Even the cat's in a crummy mood."

"What kind of way is *that* to talk?" asks my father.

"But mother said—"

"And what do you mean, '*even* the cat'?"

"Nothing," I say.

My father looks at me and shakes open his newspaper to turn the page. The newspaper knocks over my glass of milk. The milk spills onto the table.

My mother groans.

My father says all the words my mother said plus some more.

The cat jumps up on the table.

Since it isn't *my* fault, I find it funny.

"Margaret!" my mother says. "Get the cat off the table and stop it!"

"But I didn't do—"

"That was no place for your milk," my dad says, dabbing at the mess with his napkin.

"That was no place for your newspaper!" I say, standing up for my rights.

"Do what your mother tells you," he says. "Or leave the table."

I sit down. It doesn't matter.

The RIGHT MOMENT has arrived.

Posing as part of a pillar, my dragon has been waiting. Now, with an ear-shattering screech, she leaps onto the chandelier, breathing fire.

It is wonderful! Those green scales, the red with gold-tipped feathered wings, her purple eyes, the jet-black smoke. I *love* my dragon.

"*Do* something!" my mother implores.

"Now Margaret," my father begins, "won't you be *reasonable, dear?*"

There is a blast of heat and dragon-laughter from above.

"Please don't make such a big fuss!" he says, grabbing the cat who has backed into the butter.

"I find this *most* unattractive!" my mother declares.

Loud snorts and lots of oily-black smoke come from my dragon. The chandelier is swaying back and forth. Pieces of plaster from the ceiling are raining down on my favorite jam, which is really a shame, I think.

When they say, "*We surrender!*" my dragon stops screeching, hops onto the refrigerator and ruffles her feathers.

"I wish you wouldn't DO that," my father says, sitting down.

I try telling them that *I* didn't do anything, my *dragon* did. But, if you want to know what I think, they aren't listening.

"Go out and get some fresh air, Margaret," my mother advises. "*Now.*"

The fresh air we go out in is foggy.

Foggy fresh air is my dragon's favorite since it reminds her of Eastern Tibet where she was born.

Tibet is where the highest mountains in the world are.

Dragons are born there because the highest mountains are closest to the sun. And dragons, in case you didn't know it, live on light.

Which is how come they breath fire, you see.

My dragon has been living on light and breathing fire ever since she was born in Eastern Tibet where dragons don't have to be invisible since there is hardly anyone around to see them.

Here, of course, it's different.

People are everywhere, watching everything—

if not live, at least on television.

So dragons have to be discreet. Discreet means hiding your True Self until the Right Moment comes along.

After the Right Moment has come and gone, my dragon fades discreetly into the fog. Passing by, people do not see her. Either they have something in their eye or their glasses need wiping, they think. They go on their way, rubbing their eyes or wiping their glasses, shaking their heads and muttering.

If you want to know what I think, people can't see what they aren't looking for.

Everyone can see the sidewalk, and nobody's bumping into garbage cans or trees or me. But since they aren't looking for a dragon, they don't see one. If they do, they tell themselves it's something else.

Unless they're children, in which case they say, "WOW!" or, "LOOK AT THAT DRAGON!" Which worries their parents who tell them they shouldn't imagine things.

If you want to know what I think, it's funny.

Take this lady here.
She wants to know why
her son is standing with
his mouth open, staring.

If she *looked* she'd see
the same dragon he does.
But she won't, so she can't.
Instead, she's screaming,
"*Say* something, Stanley!"

Stanley says, "Wow."

"What's to 'Wow' about?" she wonders.

But he doesn't seem to hear.

"Is that your dragon?" he asks me.

"Yes." I say.

"I thought so," he says.

"A fever!" his mother cries. "That's what he must have!"

"Is it a boy or a girl?" Stanley asks.

"A girl," I tell him.

"Just like me."

I ask Stanley if *he's* got a dragon, but he says, no, he never even thought of it before.

"Maybe it was something he ate for lunch," Stanley's mother murmurs and drags him off along her way.

People either see my dragon or they don't.

Trying doesn't help. Even kids who try to see my dragon can't. Like Cynthia, for example, who is all stuck up and lives next door.

I never should have told Cynthia about my dragon in the first place.

As usual, she says, "So where's that phony dragon of yours supposed to be this morning?"

I say, "My dragon's not supposed to be anywhere because she isn't phony."

"Don't you know it's impolite to lie?" Cynthia says, smiling.

Cynthia is the one *I* think is phony, but it would be impolite to say so.

"Who's lying?" I smile back.
"You are."
"No, I'm not."
"Prove it."

"I can't," I tell her. "You've got to see for yourself. But look, maybe if you blinked your eyes very quickly . . ."

"That's the dumbest thing I ever heard," says Cynthia.

If you want to know what I think, Cynthia is asking for it. So I say, "If my dragon came and pinched you, then you'd know she's real."

"You wouldn't dare!" she says.

I think about it. If Cynthia got pinched she'd tell her mother who would tell my mother who is already angry enough as it is. It wouldn't be worth it. "You're right," I tell her.

"I dare you then," she says.

Now all I can do is shrug my shoulders — another Right Moment has arrived.

Jumping way high in the air, Cynthia shrieks. Then, grabbing her backside, she looks around, sees nothing, and turns to where I am standing still.

Even though I say I'm sorry and anyway it wasn't *me*, Cynthia goes stomping off to tell her mother.

Her mother tells my mother who was angry enough as it is and has now become angrier than ever.

If you want to know what I think, having a dragon can be difficult.

I'm going to a psychologist! That's a kind of doctor who isn't really a doctor so you don't have to take off your clothes.

His name is Dr. Rabinowitz.

I don't have to do anything I don't want to, Dr. Rabinowitz says. I say I know that, my father told me.

"What else did your father tell you?" Dr. Rabinowitz asks.
"About the pictures you can see anything you like in." I say.
He holds one up. After a while, he says, "You look disappointed."

"That's just an ink blotch," I say, "we do them in school."
"That is what's so terrific," Dr. Rabinowitz explains. "It's just an ordinary ink blotch, yet you can see anything you like in it. If you look."
"That *is* terrific," I tell him.
He is glad that I agree and asks me if I'd like to tell him what it looks like.
"If I tell you," I say, "you'll think I'm impolite."
Dr. Rabinowitz assures me that I do not have to be polite with him, but at first I can't say that his picture reminds me of Cynthia's backside because I'm giggling too hard to talk.

Dr. Rabinowitz wishes I would share my joke with him.

So I tell him how Cynthia got herself pinched, how she told her mother who told my mother who said she didn't know what to DO with me, which is why I happen to be here.

Then he holds up more pictures and I tell him what I think they look like—a face, a spider, a tree.

"No dragons?" he asks.
"Have you seen any?" I'd like to know.
"No," he says. "But that doesn't necessarily mean they don't exist."
"Good," I tell him. "Because they do."
"Well, I certainly won't ask you to prove it," Dr. Rabinowitz laughs.

It would be difficult, I explain, since my dragon is discreet.
Dr. Rabinowitz thinks that is very considerate of her.

Which makes me wonder if my dragon might not be better off in
Eastern Tibet where she could be her True Self all the time.
Except that she'd probably be bored without me.

Something funny has been happening to my dragon lately.
Before I even know what's going on, she is flying into frenzies, and if I don't control this behavior immediately, my mother says, there will be no TV for a week.

I can't control it immediately.
There is no TV for a week.

With no TV my dragon is bored.

Her tail is constantly twitching and puffs of smoke keep curling out of her nostrils.

She's always wide awake and I can tell that she is hoping for the next Right Moment to arrive as soon as possible. And it does . . .

W hen I take her to see
Dr. Rabinowitz, the doorman faints.

Smiling weakly and wiping his glasses, Dr. Rabinowitz tries not to
seem too upset.

"I had no idea she'd be so *life-like*," he tells me. "I mean, I thought
you said she was *discreet*."

"She *was*," I whisper, "only I think maybe she decided not to be so
considerate any more."

"But what does that *mean?!*" he cries.

"That it's better not to raise your voice," I tell him.

He apologizes in a whisper.

I explain that now my dragon wants to be her True Self all the time.
"Tell her it's out of the question," he says.
"Do you really want me to say that?"
He grins uneasily at my dragon who answers his look with a hiss.
"But she *can't* be her True Self all the time," he whispers.
"Why not?"
"Because it would make people uncomfortable."
"Are you uncomfortable?"
"No," he lies. "But I love animals."

My dragon has been around for quite a long time now, and it is getting on my mother's nerves.

Also, she is unhappy because everything is dusty due to the smoke always curling out of my dragon's nostrils.

If you want to know what I think, the curly smoke my dragon breathes is better to watch than television.

But my mother doesn't see it this way. What she sees is all the dust all over the furniture all the time.

The dust all over the furniture is making my father sneeze.

Sneezing all the time makes my father uncomfortable.
Also, our house is hot.
The wallpaper is puckering on the walls.
Candles are melting.
My goldfish died.

One evening my parents decide that they're going away in the morning. Without me.

Where they're going is up in the mountains, because up in the mountains they can breath some fresh air.

If you want to know what I think, no one could blame them. But I do.

More restless than ever, my dragon is flapping her wings now, as well as twitching her tail, and she is smoking so much that even I have tears in my eyes.

"Margaret," my father says. "Please don't make a big fuss."

"Who *me*?"

"Try to understand," pleads my mother, putting things into a suit-case.

I say that I'm trying.

But the truth is, I'm watching my dragon who is crouched in the corner about to leap into life, breathing fire.

Because the truth is, she's never *been* like this before. She is shaking all over, rattling her scales so sparks fly, and believe it or not, she is *humming*.

Here's what I think.

The last Right Moment has arrived!

With a shriek, I leap on my dragon as she takes off like a shooting star.

Rocketing around the room, I hear my mother wishing my father would do something, *anything*, IMMEDIATELY. But my father, who is yelling all those words you're not even supposed to say, doesn't listen.

I'm hanging on with all my might as my dragon swoops to avoid a lamp and knocks into a table so that a vase filled with daisies spills into the suitcase.

Sounding like a jet, she soars through an archway and starts circling the dining room.

Sneezing, my father follows and screams at the cat, who, with her hair standing on end, resembles a porcupine clinging to the curtains.

Through a roar in my ears I hear dishes crashing and my mother yelling into the telephone for Dr. Rabinowitz to *HURRY*.

When he comes, I'm still riding high on my dragon who is flying in fiery figure eights, hissing horribly. Terrified, Dr. Rabinowitz tells my parents to act as though nothing is happening.

My father wonders if he's out of his mind.

This hurts Dr. Rabinowitz's feelings, and he wants to know why my parents called him up in the first place if they do not want his advice.

"Don't be silly!" my father shouts. "How can we act like nothing is happening when our *daughter is destroying the dining room?!*"

"Don't be rude to Dr. Rabinowitz!" my mother cries. "He might be our only hope!"

I want to tell them not to be angry, that it will all be over in a moment, but my dragon is flying so fast it would be dangerous to do so.

Anyway, soon everyone forgets to be upset about my dragon because they're feeling so unfriendly toward each other.

They do not even see her stop.

Or notice how she hovers in mid-air—flames flowering from her nostrils, thunder rumbling in her throat.

Nobody sees me slide off her back or land on the mantle.
They do not watch us wave goodbye.

I stand by the window watching my dragon disappear until I'm so tired they have to carry me to bed.

Nobody is angry anymore. When they wonder what happened I explain that my dragon is gone for good.

"Because," I say, "even though Tibet is far away, if you want to know what I think, I'll tell you."

They say they want to know what I think.

So I tell them that waiting for the Right Moment to arrive isn't nearly as good as being your True Self all the time.

"Is that so?" they say.

"Yes," I assure them. "Especially if you're a dragon. Dragons *hate* to be discreet."

THE END

Winifred Rosen was born in 1943 and grew up in New York City to which she has recently returned after wandering around the world.

This is her ninth book for children.

Edward Koren is a well-known artist whose cartoons appear regularly in *The New Yorker* and whose drawings have been widely exhibited. Among his many books is DO YOU WANT TO TALK ABOUT IT?, a collection of his cartoons.

LIBRARY OF CONGRESS CATALOGING IN PUBLICATION DATA

Casey, Winifred Rosen, 1943— DRAGONS HATE TO BE DISCREET. *Summary: A little girl has her very own dragon*
[1. Emotions—Fiction] I. Koren, Edward. II. Title. PZ7.C26815Dr 1978 [E] 77-13867
ISBN 0-394-83577-8 ISBN 0-394-95377-2 lib. bdg.